STAR WARS ™

BEHIND THE SCENES STORIES

AND BUILD-A-SCENE INSTRUCTIONS

BENJAMIN HARPER

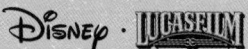

Brimming with creative inspiration, how-to projects, and useful information to enrich your everyday life, Quarto Knows is a favorite destination for those pursuing their interests and passions. Visit our site and dig deeper with our books into your area of interest: Quarto Creates, Quarto Cooks, Quarto Homes, Quarto Lives, Quarto Drives, Quarto Explores, Quarto Gifts, or Quarto Kids.

𝒟𝒾𝓈𝓃𝑒𝓎 · LUCASFILM

First Published in 2017 by becker&mayer! books, an imprint of The Quarto Group
11120 NE 33rd Place, Suite 101
Bellevue, WA 98004
www.QuartoKnows.com

This book is part of the *Star Wars Master Models: Scenes* kit and is not to be sold separately.

becker&mayer! books titles are also available at discount for retail, wholesale, promotional, and bulk purchase. For details, contact the Special Sales Manager by email at specialsales@quarto.com or by mail at The Quarto Group, Attn: Special Sales Manager, 401 Second Avenue North, Suite 310, Minneapolis, MN 55401 USA.

17 18 19 20 21 5 4 3 2 1

ISBN: 978-0-7603-5503-9

Library of Congress Cataloging-in-Publication Data available upon request.

Author: Benjamin Harper
Paper Engineer: Claudio Dias
Design: Sam Dawson
Editorial: Delia Greve
Production: Tom Miller

Printed, manufactured, and assembled in China, 07/17.

MIX
Paper from
responsible sources
FSC® C017606

171043

CONTENTS

SETTING THE SCENE

Since that moment in 1977 when audiences first witnessed Princess Leia's ship, *Tantive IV*, being chased over the desert planet of Tatooine by a giant, looming Star Destroyer, people around the world have been fascinated by the vast tale of the Skywalker family, the downfall of the Republic and the rise of the Empire, and the battle between the light and dark sides of the Force, the energy field that connects all living things.

Behind the scenes of the *Star Wars* galaxy, film wizardry takes place. In order to bring George Lucas's vision to the screen, special effects experts worked tirelessly, trying new and modified techniques to make every action, ship, planet, creature, explosion, and lightsaber as lifelike and believable as possible. What comes off as effortless and dazzling on the screen actually

ABOVE: Darth Vader pursues Princess Leia above the desert planet of Tatooine as she tries to deliver stolen Death Star plans to the Rebel Alliance.

took whole teams of dedicated people to create. In fact, George Lucas's crew invented some of the techniques they used as the films were being made!

And although technology changed drastically between the making of *A New Hope* and the completion of *The Force Awakens*, many of the original methods for producing the effects were employed throughout the series. Indeed, some of the practical effects created for the original trilogy have been brought back for the latest *Star Wars* film.

Iconic action scenes would not have been the same without creative thinking and on-the-spot innovation, and nowhere is that more evident than in the three key moments—one from each trilogy—presented in this kit. Take a look at the behind-the-scenes secrets that create the on-screen wonder!

STAR WARS: EPISODE III REVENGE OF THE SITH

The Dark Side vs. The Light Side: The Battle on Mustafar

Darkness had engulfed the galaxy. Chancellor Palpatine had declared himself Emperor of the new Galactic Empire and had also secretly taken a Sith apprentice: former Jedi Knight Anakin Skywalker. Anakin turned to the dark side when he was led to believe it was the only way to save his wife Padmé from a death he had foreseen.

In his first act as Darth Vader, Anakin marched on the Jedi Temple and killed all Jedi he encountered. He then flew to the molten planet Mustafar to eliminate the Separatist leaders who had been using the planet as a hideout. The act would officially end the civil war, and the Sith would rule the galaxy.

ABOVE: Jedi Master Obi-Wan Kenobi and his former apprentice, Anakin Skywalker, clash in a battle of light against dark on the molten planet of Mustafar.

Master Yoda had ordered Obi-Wan Kenobi to find and destroy his former apprentice. Obi-Wan knew the quickest way to locate the new Sith was to confront Padmé, whom he knew would rush to Anakin. Stowed away on Padmé's ship, Obi-Wan arrives on Mustafar.

As Padmé begs Anakin to come away with her to raise the child they were expecting and Anakin reveals his plan to rule the galaxy, Obi-Wan exits Padmé's ship. Anakin accuses his wife of bringing the Jedi with her. Enraged, Anakin Force chokes his wife into unconsciousness. With lightsaber drawn, Anakin confronts Obi-Wan.

The battle rages on the landing platform, but Anakin forces his former master back into the inner rooms of the Mustafarian mining complex. Scattered all around the dueling Jedi and Sith lay the crumpled bodies of Separatist leaders and dignitaries, grim testaments to Anakin's rapid descent into the dark side.

As they fight through the complex, the two launch themselves at each other, lightsabers clashing. Using all the strength and will their knowledge of the Force grants them, the two battle, equally matched. Using Force pushes and lightsaber slashes, their fight compromises the system that controls the protective repulsor fields that keep the mining complex from melting in the extreme volcanic heat of Mustafar.

The collapse of the facility does not deter their battle. Out on an observation balcony, lava bubbles and explodes all around them. Eventually they end up balancing across deadly service ducts that run across the molten river to a giant collector arm. Without the fields' protection, the suspension wires holding the arm in place melt, toppling the structure into the molten river. The two continue their fight as they float down the flow toward a lava fall, balanced on a hovering mining platform and a small collector droid.

Anakin flips from the droid and onto Obi-Wan's platform. Finally, Obi-Wan leaps onto the riverbank, gaining the high ground. Anakin refuses to believe he could be defeated. In a foolhardy move, Anakin jumps off the platform toward Obi-Wan, who slices through his former apprentice's legs, leaving him critically wounded on the fiery shore of the lava river.

Too emotionally distraught to deal the final blow against his former friend and Padawan, Obi-Wan leaves Anakin to his fate and rushes back to help Padmé, not knowing what Anakin would soon become.

How it Was Filmed

It took teams of people months of work to put together the extremely complex sequences that make up this decisive battle between Obi-Wan Kenobi and Anakin Skywalker on the molten planet. What races by quickly on the screen passed through several departments working together to create the effect of real lava and the thrill of an epic duel that used Force powers, leaps, lightsabers, and plenty of

ABOVE: Concept art sets the scene for this epic battle. Actors Hayden Christensen and Ewan McGregor duel in front of green screen before final effects are dropped in.

explosions. In fact, some sequences that are seen only for seconds on-screen took a crew weeks or even months to complete.

First, Hayden Christensen and Ewan McGregor, the actors who portrayed Anakin Skywalker and Obi-Wan Kenobi, had to take part in rigorous training to make their sword fighting look realistic. Although they were performing in front of a green screen, their choreographed flips and kicks were very much real, and in most cases they performed their own stunts.

The sequence was initially mapped out in storyboards, based on George Lucas's vision for the battle. He reviewed each sketch and made comments until the sequence was exactly what he wanted it to be. Then the entire fight was created in animatics—rough animations that gave the special effects crews an idea of the vision they would be bringing to the screen and also established a starting point for building the various sets and components required to make the sequence come to life. Everything from the droids that floated over the lava river to the panels in the Separatist boardroom was planned to exact specifications.

In some cases, full-size practical sets were built for such locations as the Mustafar landing platform and Separatist base. Walls behind the pieces were painted green in order to create composite effects later on. Some of the moving pieces were filmed on practical sets as well, such as the floating platform Obi-Wan rides down the lava river. The raised platform was surrounded by green screen, and circular track was laid around its base. A model of the floating droid Anakin balances on was placed on the track. When the shoot took place, Hayden Christensen stood on the track as it rolled around the platform.

In order to make practical sets and computer-generated effects sync up in final shots, 3D matchmovers placed targets on the blue or green screens the actors or models were filmed against. These targets were necessary in order to make sure that computer-generated backgrounds and effects would match perspectives and camera angles when composited into the shots. When effects crews reviewed the green or blue screen shots, they could tell by the marker placement on the screen how the camera was panning or how the action was moving and used special software that locates the targets and creates a virtual environment that matches the shots. Then they were able to create a virtual replica of what was filmed so other departments could create backgrounds, environments, or actions to match real-life movements and incorporate them into the final shots.

The backgrounds and environments that were dropped in were digital matte paintings, some of which incorporated real-world elements, such as volcano eruptions, lava flows, or giant billows of smoke. Other elements were modified, such as gravel, employed to create the illusion of lava flows. Background paintings were created as giant landscapes, and then animated, so they would appear as real environments in the film. The intricacies of the backdrops meant it took several months to complete just one.

Animators had the immense task of bringing the epic scale of the Mustafar battle to life. The monstrous collector arm that toppled into the molten river while Obi-Wan and Anakin were battling on it is a perfect example of the work the animation department did for the scene. Nothing in the effect is practical—from the arm tumbling into the deadly flow to the Jedi keeping balance and racing toward its tip for safety, lightsaber flashing, the entire piece is computer-generated.

The incredible lava effects appearing in the scene were achieved in many different ways. First, footage from an explosion at the active volcano Mount Etna in Sicily, Italy, was incorporated in various places. Second, a compound called methylcellulose, which is gel-like in consistency, was underlit with colored lights and used in practical flows to create the effect of liquid lava. Sprays of methylcellulose were also filmed and then colored digitally to create spurts and blasts of lava shooting upward. Each instance of lava that appeared in the shot was then digitally lit to give it a 3D effect.

Digital modelers created digital versions of every single element seen in the sequence and had to make them exceedingly detailed. Elements such as the massive collector arm had to be detailed not only on the outside, but also in the interior, because it breaks away from its anchor and floats down the river. These modelers spent many weeks creating digital versions of objects seen in the movie for only a split second.

Although digital elements exist in every second of the duel on Mustafar, practical effects were also used. A scale model of the Mustafar surface was created by the effects crew and built on a giant wooden base that could tilt at different angles to control and change the speed and direction of the lava flow. In between the rocky mountains on the surface where the lava river coursed was a clear base that could be under lit to create an igneous glow in the river. Once again, lava was created by using colored methylcellulose. When the liquid was poured into the river basin and under lit, it looked like flowing lava. The addition of smoke, steam, and sparks gave the miniature set an even greater air of reality.

Once all the separate special effects elements for the Mustafar sequence were completed and approved, compositors took the individual components and combined them into what would become the final film frame. The final composited film was then sent to the sound designers, who added all the riveting audio effects—from lightsaber blades clashing to actor voiceovers.

When each layer was in place, the scene was edited into a final mix, bringing to life the tragedy of Anakin's final descent into the dark side, from which he would emerge as Darth Vader.

ABOVE: Early concept art gives set builders an idea of what they will need to create to deliver the dazzling final sequence.

Tools and materials you'll need

Craft knife (X-Acto knife)

White glue

12" ruler

Colored markers or pencils

Tweezers

Paintbrush

Useful tips

- Completely read these instructions before starting. Make sure you understand all instructions.
- Detach pieces carefully as they are needed.
- Avoid overapplication of glue! This may cause paper to wrinkle. Use a paintbrush to apply glue.
- For these instructions, printed surfaces are shown in gray and non-printed in white.
- Use the white areas and yellow lines printed on the pieces to help align pieces when gluing.
- When you detach pieces, white edges will be apparent. Use a marker or pencil to color these edges before gluing them.
- **Mountain fold** means to fold the paper so the printed surface is facing out.
- **Valley fold** means to fold the paper so the printed surface is facing in.
- Remove pieces marked with a red star (∗).
- When building, be sure the glue dries completely before proceeding to the next step.
- When joining two pieces, start by gluing the tabs marked with a green star (∗).
- When joining opened pieces, such as partial cones or cylinders, start by gluing two tabs. When completely dry, glue the remaining tabs.

THE BATTLE ON MUSTAFAR
BUILDING INSTRUCTIONS

BOX

- Fold piece B1 as shown and glue it to the inside top edge of piece B2.

- Mountain fold the tabs on pieces B3 and B4 and glue them to B1 and B2 as shown to form the box. Note: For this scene use the B4 piece with the small hole.

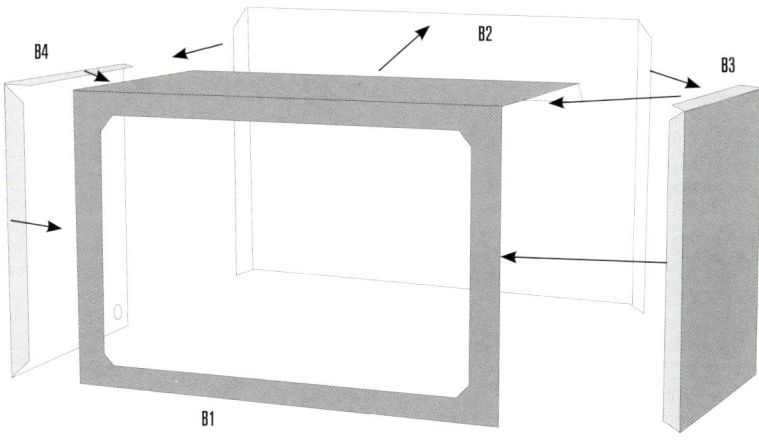

NOTE: For the following instructions, use pieces from the sheets labeled "The Battle on Mustafar."

BRIDGE

- Assemble pieces 13 and 14 to form open box shapes as shown and mountain fold all tabs. Repeat four more times so there are five sets.

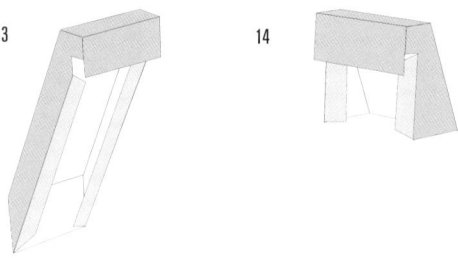

- Form piece 10 into a U-shape as shown. Glue the five sets of piece 13 to one side of piece 10 and the five sets of piece 14 to the other. Use the lines on piece 10 to align them.

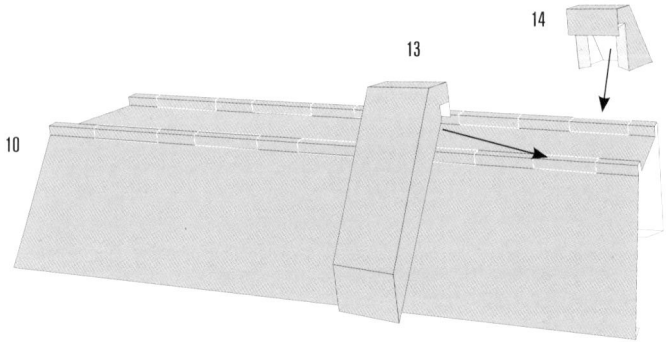

BUILDING STRUCTURE

- Fold piece 9 into the structure as shown and mountain fold all tabs. Glue piece 9 to the non-printed side of piece 8.

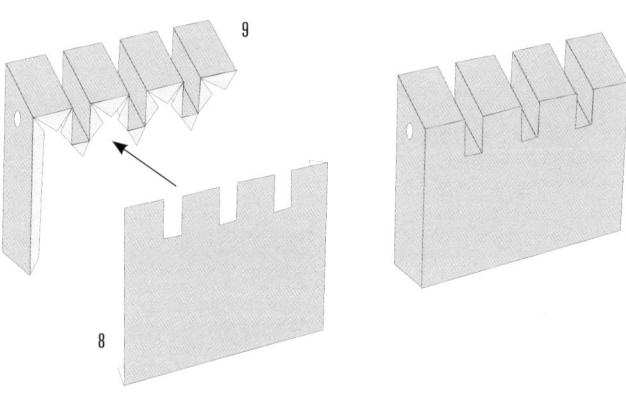

MOUNTAIN

- Glue the piece of vellum paper behind piece 6. Tip: Trace the shape of piece 6 onto the vellum paper, cut it out, and glue in place. Or cut strips of vellum and glue them behind each slit on piece 6. Then mountain fold the tabs on piece 6.

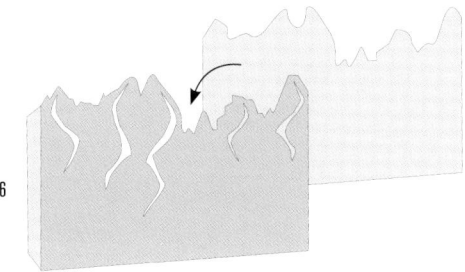

SCENE FRAME

- Valley fold the tabs on pieces 1, 2, 4, and 5.

- Glue each side of piece 2 to a side tab on piece 4 and 5 as shown so the printed surfaces all face in.

- Glue piece 1 to the bottom of the structure formed by pieces 2, 4, and 5, so all printed surfaces are facing in.

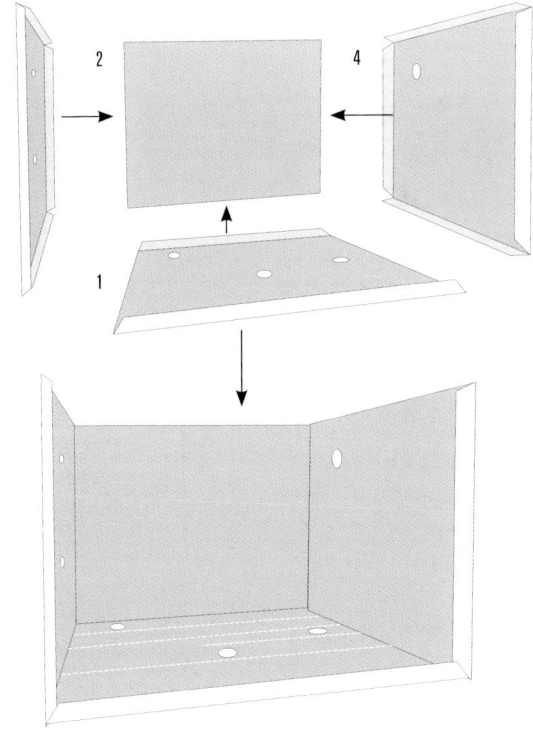

- Align the bottom tab of piece 6 with the line marked farthest back on piece 1 and glue the tab in place so the printed side faces out. Then, gently fold it back, and glue the side tabs to pieces 4 and 5, aligning the printed edge with the lines on those pieces.

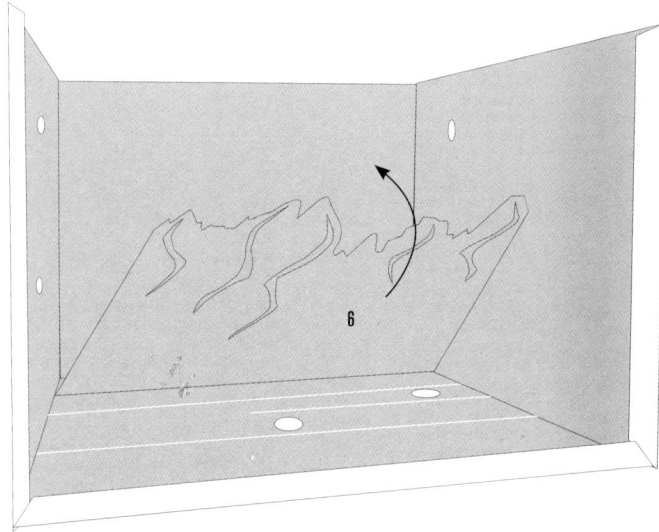

- Repeat this step using piece 7, aligning it to the guide line in front of piece 6.
- Glue the building structure to align with the next guide line. This piece will sit to the right and attach only to the side of piece 4. Next, glue the bridge into position, using the line mark as a guide for the back edge of the piece. The front edge of the bridge should come to the front edge of piece 1.

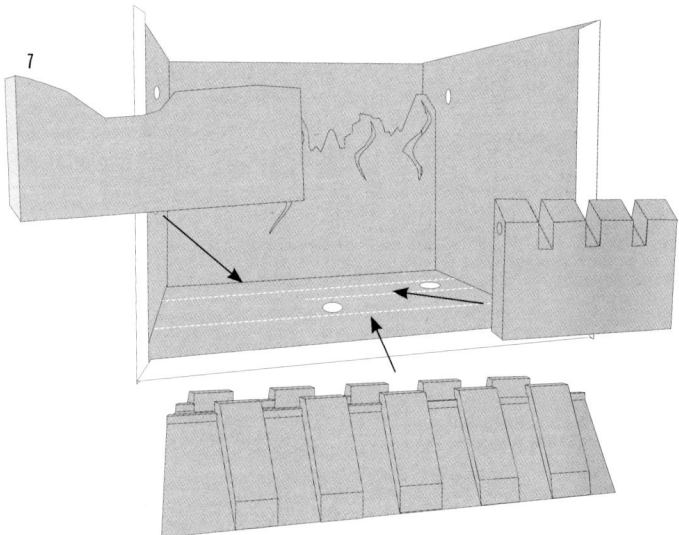

PIPES

- Assemble pieces 11 and 12 to form cylinders as shown.

12

11

- Slide piece 12 through the top hole in piece 5 so it extends across the scene and then insert it into the hole on piece 4. Add some glue to the external side of piece 5 to hold the pipe in place.
- Slide piece 11 through the bottom hole in piece 5 so it extends across to building structure and then insert it into the hole on piece 9. Add some glue on the external side of piece 5 to hold the pipe to it.

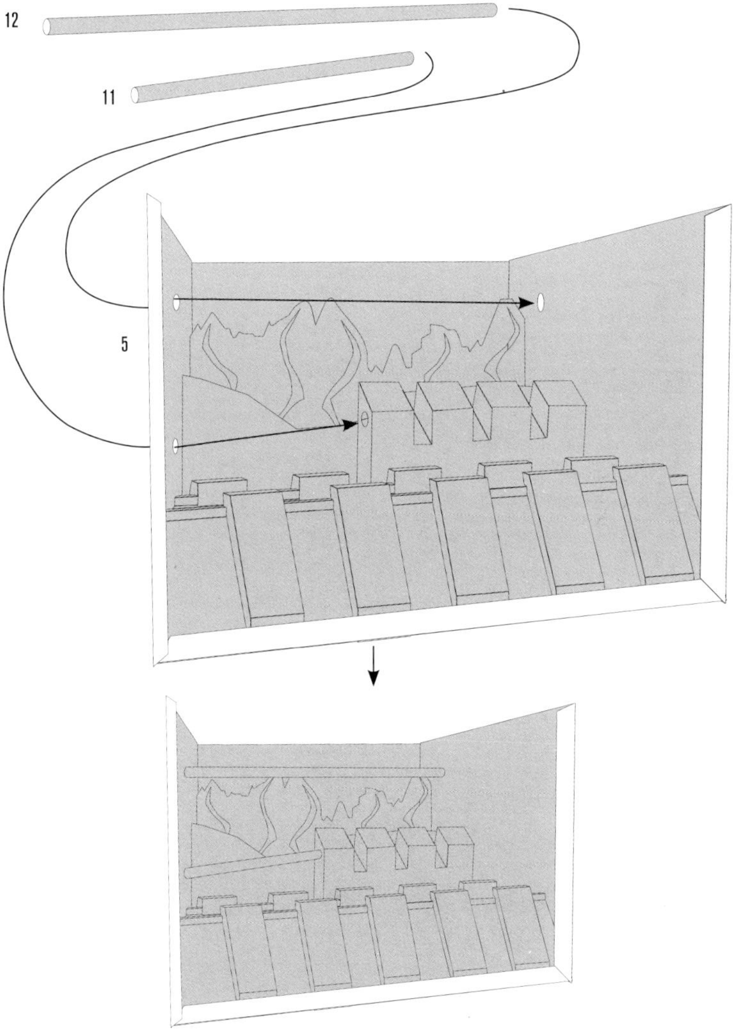

12

11

5

ANAKIN AND OBI-WAN

- Fold piece 19 in half and valley fold all tabs. Glue the center shut. Repeat so you have two pieces.

- Glue one piece 19 behind Anakin's leg and the other one behind Obi-Wan's leg as shown.

- Glue piece 18 behind Anakin's hands, keeping the angle as shown. Glue piece 16 behind Obi-Wan's hands again in the angle shown.

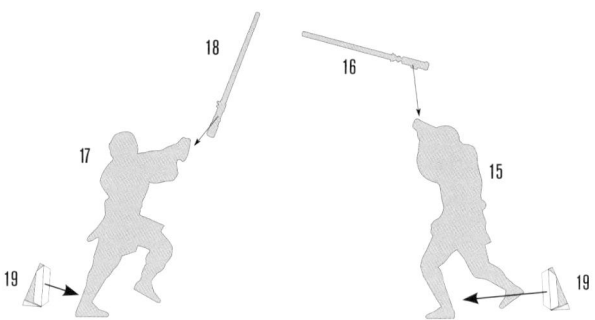

- Glue both characters onto the bridge at the center. Make sure they are close enough for their lightsabers to cross.

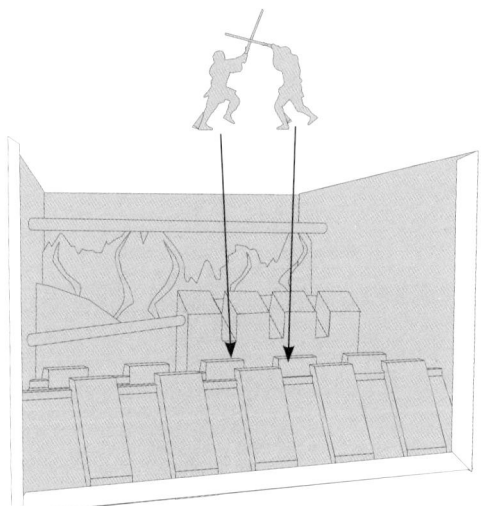

FINAL ASSEMBLY

- Valley fold the tabs on piece 3.

- Glue piece 3 to the top of the structure formed by pieces 2, 4, and 5. This completes the scene frame.

- Insert the scene frame into the outer box so the scene shows through the opening. Glue the tabs highlighted in yellow to the inside of the window of the box.

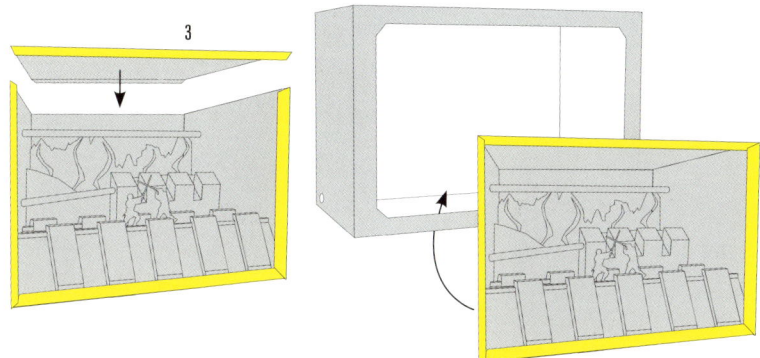

LIGHT MODULE

- Assemble piece 22 to form a triangular box as shown. Place piece 22 into the bottom corner of the outer box, with the flat side facing up, and align the hole in piece 22 with the hole on the side of the box. Glue in place.

- Assemble piece 20 to form a box as shown, keeping the end with the two tabs open. Insert the module into piece 20 so the wires stick out the side. Glue the box shut.

- Using a craft knife, cut along the two "X" marks on piece 21. Open the X's up a little and press the knobs on the back of the button chip into the holes. Fit the gray button into the hole in piece 22 so it sticks out of the outer box. Glue piece 21 to the inside of piece 22 to hold the button in place. Thread the wire through the slit on the opposite side of piece 22.

- Insert the three lights into the corresponding holes on the bottom of the scene frame.

- Glue piece 20 with the module to the bottom of the scene frame at the back of the outer box. Be sure the battery access door is facing out. Last, adjust the lights as desired and tape or glue the wires to the under side of the scene frame.

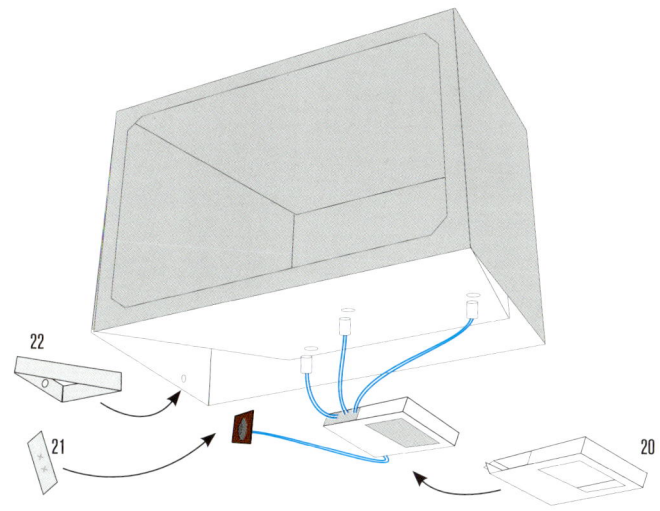

The Rebellion Turns the Tide: The Battle of Yavin

It was a desperate time for the Rebellion. Princess Leia had escaped the Death Star with stolen tactical plans, but the Empire had tracked her escape aboard the *Millennium Falcon* and discovered the rebels' secret base on a moon orbiting the planet Yavin.

As the planet-destroying Death Star orbited the gas giant Yavin, moving ever closer to the rebel base, the freedom fighters organized a last-ditch attack to save their lives and rid the galaxy of the Death Star. The plans Princess Leia had supplied revealed a glitch in the space station's design —a small exhaust port in the meridian trench could, if hit directly with a

ABOVE: Rebel X-wing pilots begin their risky assault on the Empire's dreaded Death Star.

proton torpedo, cause a chain reaction within the station's core that would destroy it.

As Princess Leia and other rebel leaders monitor the Death Star's approach from a command center on Yavin 4's surface, X-wing and Y-wing fighters blast off into space in preparation for battle. Among the freedom fighters to risk their lives in the fight is young Luke Skywalker with the loyal droid R2-D2 in his X-wing astromech socket.

The rebel ships are so small they are able to evade the Death Star's turbolasers. Thus, Darth Vader orders his troops to their ships, and the Imperials launch droves of TIE fighters to battle the rebel's fighters in a dogfight.

As small Imperial and rebel craft battle along the extensive surface of the space station, the rebels focus on thinning out the Imperial fighters before beginning their trench runs, and time is running out. As each second passes, the Death Star moves closer and closer to the rebel base.

In the first attempt at an attack run, the Y-wings descend into the trench and race toward the exhaust port, their targeting computers locked. They maneuver through blasts from turbolasers when suddenly the cannons stop their attacks. Darth Vader, flanked by two other TIE fighters, joins the battle himself and flies into the trench after the Y-wings. Each Y-wing falls prey to the Imperials, unable to complete their attack.

The leader of the X-wing squadron commands Luke and two other X-wing pilots to cover them as another group of X-wing pilots began their run. Darth Vader once again slips into the trench, taking out one of the X-wings. The leader is able to fire off a proton torpedo, but it misses the target.

It is up to Luke, his friend Biggs, and rebel pilot Wedge to make a third attempt. Vader once again follows the X-wings into the trench. Wedge is hit and has to evacuate, but Darth Vader keeps his focus on the two remaining pilots in the trench.

With thirty seconds to go until the Death Star is in range of the rebel base, Luke hears the voice of his mentor Obi-Wan Kenobi telling him to trust in the Force.

As Luke heeds Obi-Wan's guidance, Darth Vader takes aim. Out of nowhere, the *Millennium Falcon* soars to the scene, firing on one of Darth Vader's wingmen, causing Darth Vader's TIE fighter to spin off into space.

Luke focuses on the Force and fires. His proton torpedoes hit their target, and the remaining rebels evacuate as the Death Star explodes. Although they deal a blow to the Empire, the war is far from over.

How It Was Filmed

The special effects crew that worked on the original *Star Wars* film was tasked with bringing George Lucas's vision to the screen, both on time and on budget. And in order to do so they had to be inventive. In no other scene of the film is that more evident than in the epic and frenetic final battle that takes place above the surface of the enormous Death Star.

Before filming of the sequences began, they were mapped out in storyboards to define each ship's placement and battle action with the scene. Once Lucas gave the final OK on a scene, filming could begin. Some action was ultimately too difficult to convey in standard storyboards, so Lucas cut together a film sequence of the battle using old World War II footage and war scenes from old films. Although the action that he pieced together for the special effects experts to review was a lot slower than what he expected for the final film, it gave the crew an idea of the physical movements he wanted for the fight scenes and a starting point in the reality of aerial combat on which to base the battle. After the sequences were finalized in story-boards, work began on bringing them to the screen—a challenging but exciting task for the talented crew.

Nothing is more noticeable in the Battle of Yavin than the enormous, terrifying Death Star. In order to make the space station effective in various shots, many different types of physical models were necessary. First, matte paintings of its surface were created, which were used in sequences that did not demand any changes to perspective. For establishing shots, a full model—about four feet across—was built.

The actual battle sequences that occurred above the surface of the Death Star and within the trench leading to the exhaust port took a variety of models as well. Large modules built from model components were put together on giant panels and could be fitted together in different combinations to create varying arrangements of surface details for close-up shots. From those, a smaller surface was also created, pasting photographs of the models onto a curved board for use in distance shots. A giant model of the trench was built for flyover and explosion shots, using a camera on a track to create the flying effects.

The TIE fighters, X-wings, and Y-wings were all custom-built models. Each was approximately one and a half to two feet wide. In order to create the illusion of flight, the ships were shot using motion-control cameras in front of a blue screen. The use of a new all-digital camera called a Dykstraflex (named after Industrial Light & Magic [ILM] special-effects artist John Dykstra) allowed for multiple axes of motion—including rolling, panning, tilting, tracking, and more—that gave the models the appearance of soaring effortlessly through space. After completing the initial shots of the models, they were composited onto a starfield background along with the Death Star.

Exploding ships in space were filmed in front of a blue screen. Tiny explosive charges were placed inside the vehicles, and as cameras focused in on the models, the charges were detonated. When they were composited over the space back-ground, the ships had the appearance of being shot down in battle.

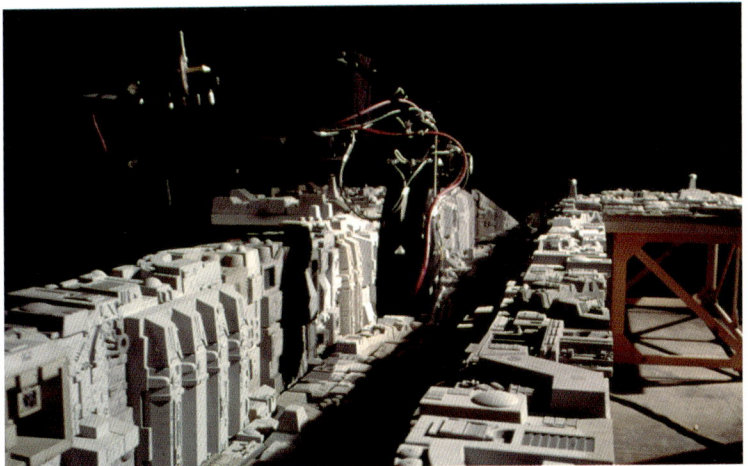

TOP: The model of the Death Star's trench. **BELOW:** Filming explosions on the space station's surface.

The race to the exhaust port at the end of the Death Star trench—that tense scene in which the audience learns just how powerful the Force can be—was filmed to give the appearance of ships racing at top speed, the sides of the trench whizzing by in a blur. Filming the trench battle sequences involved running a camera along a track through the giant trench model. The Dykstraflex camera was used to create the views from the pilots' cockpits as the ships swerved and swayed to miss oncoming blasts from the Death Star's defense systems and blasts from Darth Vader as he pursued fleeing rebel craft. Model ships were filmed flying and exploding in front of a green screen. The shots were composited together to create the amazingly tense sequence that appears in the movie.

Of course, the most important action of the Battle of Yavin comes when Luke Skywalker blasts proton torpedoes directly into the station's vulnerable exhaust port, causing it to explode. Wanting to create a truly sensational image, they shot the explosion looking directly up onto a model of the space station, using a high-speed camera. When the detonation occurred, debris continued to rain down after the explosion, creating the appearance of burning fragments of metal flying away from the blast.

Once all these different components were finalized and composited into a cohesive sequence, they were sent for sound mixing and dubbing. George Lucas and his team worked arduous hours to finalize the sequence, bringing the legendary Battle of Yavin to the screen.

OPPOSITE: A model of the Death Star's surface used for low pass shots. **ABOVE:** The ILM special effects crew poses with a panel of the Death Star.

THE TRENCH RUN
BUILDING INSTRUCTIONS

BOX

- Fold piece B1 as shown and glue it to the inside top edge of piece B2.

- Mountain fold the tabs on pieces B3 and B4 and glue them to B1 and B2 as shown above to form the box.

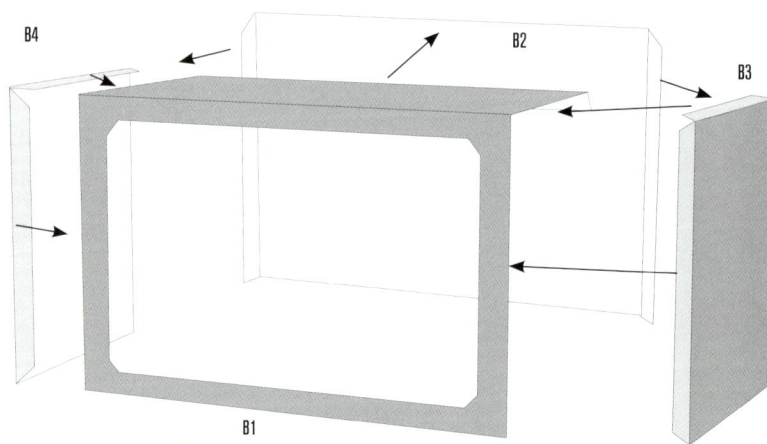

NOTE: For the following instructions, use pieces from the sheets labeled "The Trench Run."

X-WING FUSELAGE

- Fold pieces 1, 2, 3, 5, and 6 to form shapes as shown. Mountain fold all the tabs.
- Glue piece 1 to piece 6. Add piece 2 to this set and glue in place. Then, add piece 5 and glue in place. Last, add piece 3 and glue in place.
- Glue piece 4 to the end of piece 3 and 5 to form the X-wing fuselage.

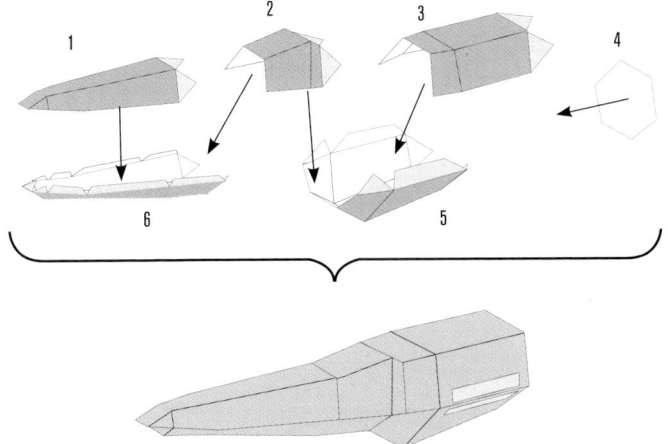

X-WING WINGS

- Fold piece 7 in half and glue the piece closed. Repeat this for piece 8.
- Assemble piece 9 and 10 to form boxes as shown.
- Glue piece 9 to piece 7—aligned with the white section on piece 7. Repeat, attaching piece 10 to the white section on piece 8.
- Repeat these steps to form two sets of wings.

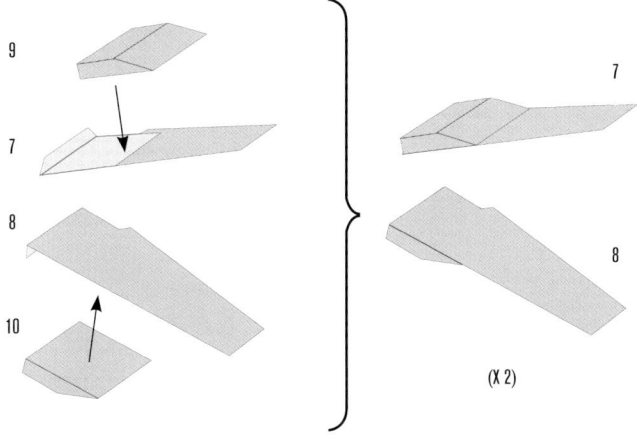

(X 2)

X-WING ENGINES

- Assemble pieces 15 and 16 to form cylinders as shown and mountain fold the tabs. Attach a piece 18 to the circular end of each as shown.

- Glue the flat part of piece 16 to the top of piece 9, so the cylinder end hangs over. Repeat, gluing the flat part of piece 15 to the top of piece 10.

- Assemble two piece 17s to form cylinders and insert the tip into the open ends of pieces 15 and 16—insert the white end and glue in place.

- Repeat the previous three steps for the other set of wings. Be sure to switch the direction the engine cylinders face on the second set of wings.

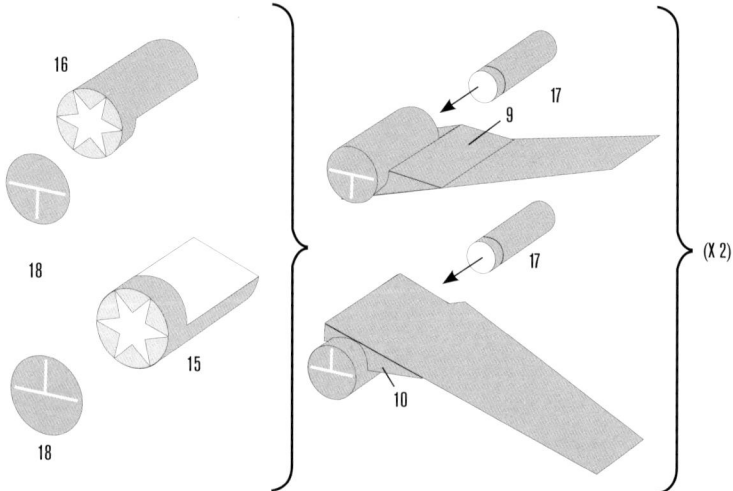

- Glue each wing to its proper position on the fuselage as shown. Use the white boxes on the fuselage as a guide.

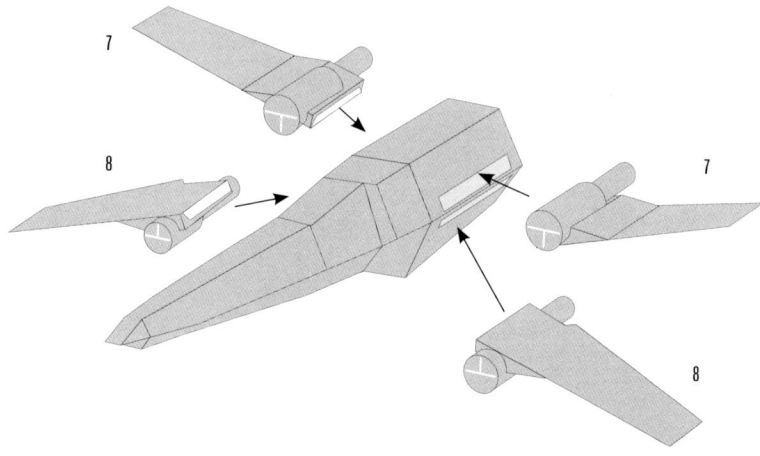

X-WING LASER GUNS

- Assemble piece 12 to form a cylinder. Wrap piece 11 around piece 12, using the white area on piece 12 as a guide.

- Fold piece 13 in half and glue closed. Once dry, shape it form a curve as shown. Glue piece 13 to the tip of piece 12.

- On piece 14, cut along the green line at the tip to form tabs. Fold piece 14 in half and mountain fold the cut tabs. Glue the piece closed making sure the tabs remain open. Glue piece 14 to the center of piece 13.

- Repeat the previous three steps three more times so there are four laser guns.

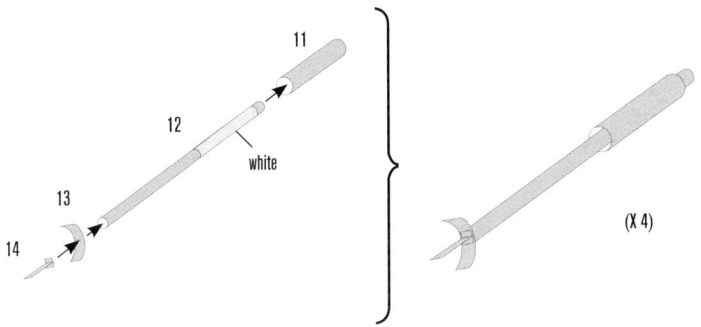

- Glue one laser to the tip of each wing, using the white boxes as a guide. Make sure all laser guns are pointing toward the fuselage with the curved laser tips vertical and are on the outside of the wings as shown.

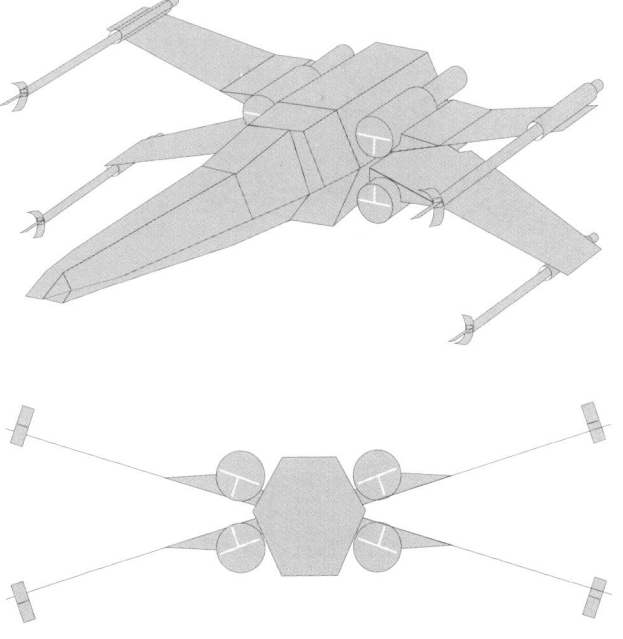

ADVANCED TIE-FIGHTER COCKPIT

- Curve pieces 19, 20, 21, and 22 slightly and mountain fold all tabs.

- Glue piece 19 to 20 and piece 21 to 22 as shown.

- Assemble pieces 23 and 24 to form cones as shown. Mountain fold the tabs on the small end, and valley fold the tabs on the large end.

- Join pieces 23 and 24 to the sets formed by pieces 19–22. Glue them in place so the tabs on 23 and 24 are inside pieces 19–22.

- Using a craft knife cut along the green lines on pieces 26 and 27 to form tabs. Assemble pieces 26 and 27 to form short cones and mountain fold the cut tabs

- Glue piece 26 above and piece 27 below the cockpit.

- Assemble pieces 25 and 28 to form cones. Glue piece 25 to the top of the cockpit and piece 28 to the bottom of the cockpit.

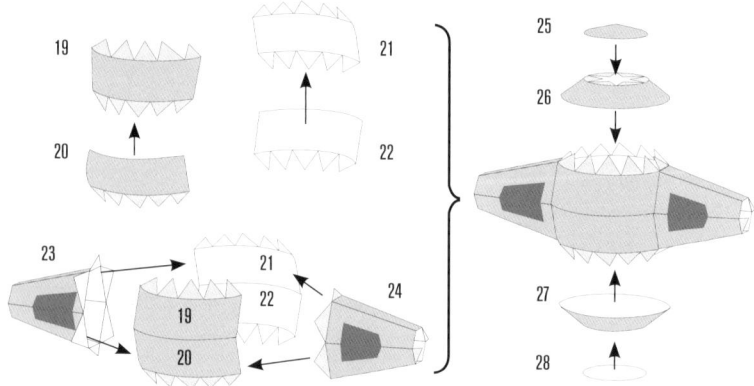

ADVANCED TIE-FIGHTER FUSELAGE

- Valley fold all tabs on the two piece 29s. Glue the two pieces together leaving the tabs open.

- Fold both piece 30s as shown, mountain folding the tabs. Glue one piece 30 to the top of piece 29 and the other to the underside of piece 29, using the white areas as a guide. This forms the fuselage.

- Glue the fuselage to the cockpit as shown, so the black window is facing forward.

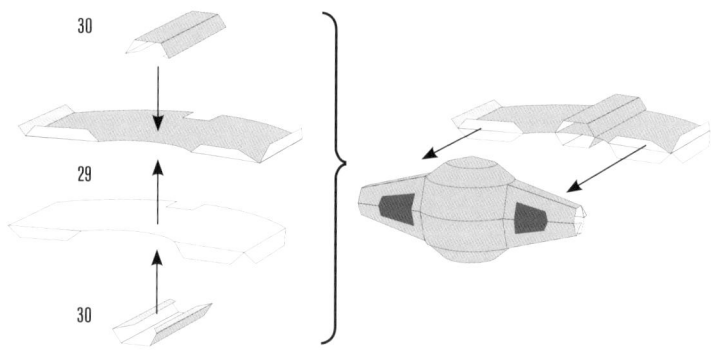

ADVANCED TIE-FIGHTER WINGS

- Fold pieces 31, 32, 33, and 34 as shown. Glue piece 32 to piece 34 and glue piece 31 to piece 33. These form the TIE fighter wings

- Glue the wings to fuselage and cockpit as shown, aligning the gray hexagons on pieces 31 and 32 with the ends of pieces 23 and 24.

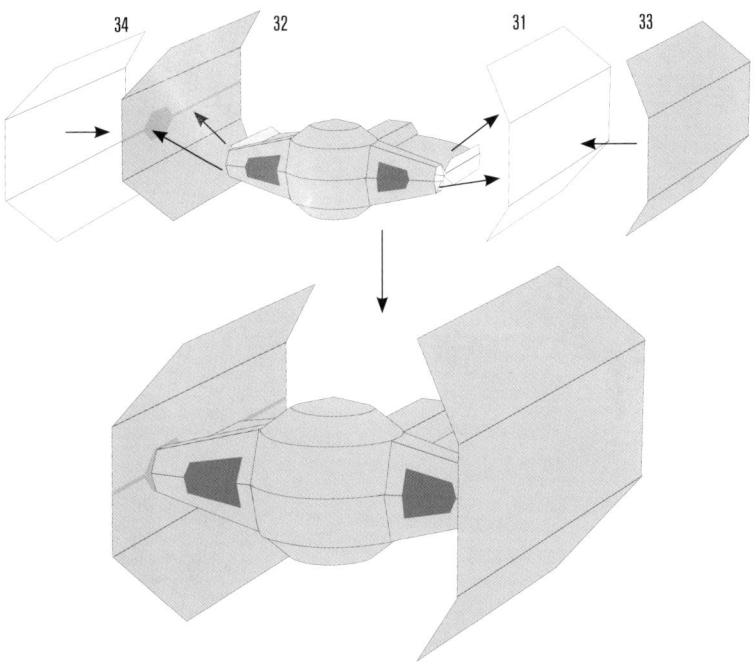

SCENE FRAME

- Valley fold the tabs on pieces 42, 44, 45, and 46.

- Glue each side of piece 42 to a side tab on piece 44 and 46 as shown, so the printed surfaces all face in.

- Glue piece 45 to the bottom of the structure formed by pieces 42, 44, and 46 so all printed surfaces are facing in.

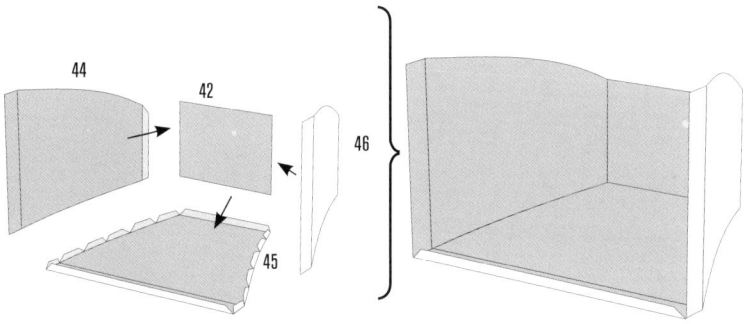

- Mountain fold the tabs on piece 37. Align the bottom tab with the line marked farthest back on piece 45 and glue in place so the printed side faces out. Then, gently fold piece 37 back and glue the side tabs to pieces 44 and 46 to align with the deepest line marks on those pieces.

- Assemble piece 36 to form a cone as shown with the tabs mountain folded. Center the wide end of the piece 36 over the white circle on piece 42 and glue in place. This will hold the Advanced TIE fighter in place.

- Position the ship so the small end of piece 36 inserts into the opening formed by piece 30. Glue piece 30 to piece 36.

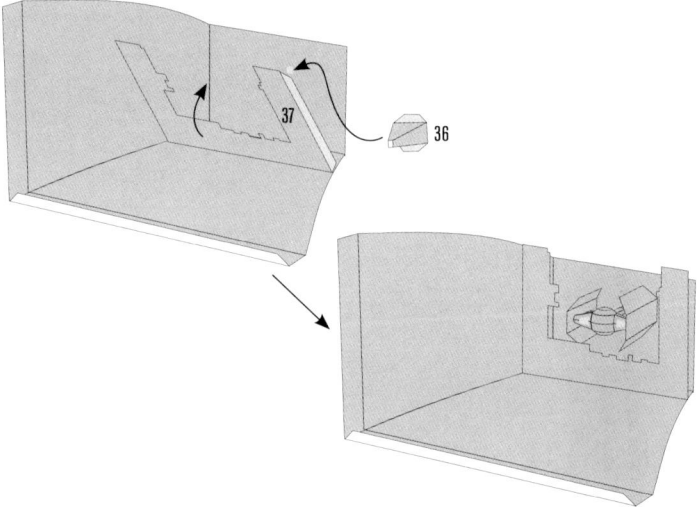

- Mountain fold the tabs on pieces 38, 39, and 40. Align the bottom tabs of each piece with the lines marked on piece 45, allowing for the increased size of each piece. Glue the tabs in place so the printed sides face out. Fold back and attach each piece to the sides of the scene frame.

- Assemble piece 35 to form a cone-shaped box and mountain fold the tabs. Glue piece 35 between pieces 39 and 40 as shown, using the white box as a guide. This will hold the X-wing starfighter.

- Position the X-wing onto the stand using the white box on the underside of the fuselage as a guide. Glue in place.

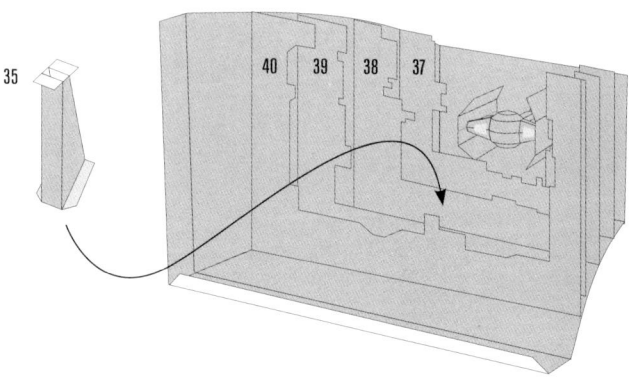

FINAL ASSEMBLY

- Mountain fold tabs on piece 41. Align the bottom tab with the remaining line on piece 45 and glue in place. Fold it back and glue the side tabs in place.

- Valley fold the tabs on piece 43.

- Glue piece 43 to the top of the structure fromed by pieces 42, 44, and 46. This completes the scene frame.

- Insert the scene frame into the outer box so the scene shows through the opening. Glue the tabs highlighted in yellow to the inside of the window of the box.

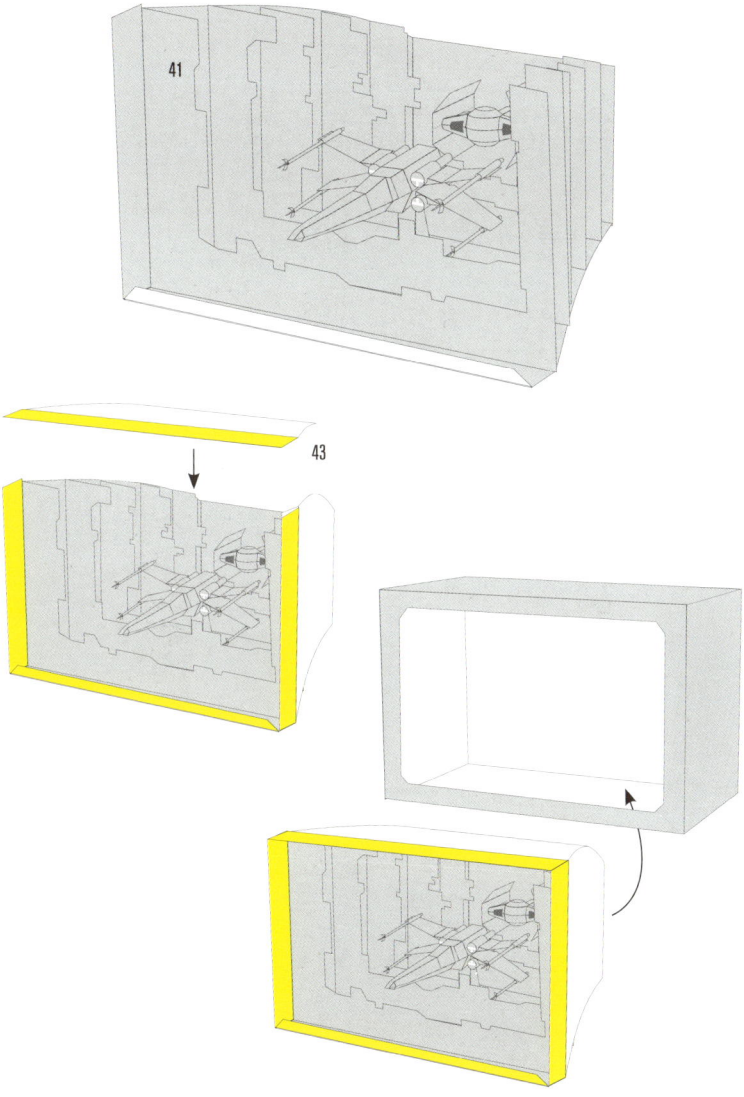

STAR WARS: EPISODE VII THE FORCE AWAKENS

The Clash of Light and Dark: Duel on Starkiller Base

Thirty years after the Rebel Alliance toppled the Galactic Empire and destroyed its dreaded second Death Star, a new evil has risen. The sinister First Order, led by Supreme Leader Snoke and his commanding officer General Hux and apprentice Kylo Ren, has set its sights on taking over the galaxy.

Kylo Ren captures the young scavenger girl Rey and takes her to the icy planet that has become Starkiller Base. There, he hopes to read her mind and extract from it the map leading to Luke Skywalker, the last of the Jedi. Luke had gone into hiding after Kylo, a former student of his, turned to the dark side and killed the new Jedi Luke had been training. With Skywalker's secret location

ABOVE: Kylo Ren and Rey battle in the snowy forest on the surface of Starkiller Base.

location in hand, Kylo Ren could hunt down the last Jedi and extinguish the light side of the Force. But something is wrong. During his interrogation, he cannot penetrate Rey's mind; the girl is powerful in the Force herself and reads *his* mind instead. Seeking guidance from Supreme Leader Snoke, Kylo Ren leaves Rey under the guard of a stormtrooper. With the Force surging through her, Rey succeeds in using a Jedi mind trick to make the stormtrooper to set her free. Loose in the First Order's base, Rey searches for a ship in order to escape the planet.

In the meantime, Han Solo, Chewbacca, and Finn fly the *Millennium Falcon* to Starkiller Base in order to lower its shields and stop it from destroying the planet where the Resistance base is located. Han Solo and Finn's success in bringing the shields down is the Resistance's only hope to defend itself against the dreaded weapon. Han, Chewbacca, and Finn take Captain Phasma prisoner and force her to lower the shield surrounding the planet. The Resistance's X-wing fighters, led by Poe Dameron, launch their attack, bombarding the thermal oscillator.

In addition to lowering the shields, Finn also planned to rescue Rey, but as they begin their search, Han spots her across a chasm, free, and climbing the wall toward a ship. The Resistance fighters race to meet up with Rey.

As they flee toward the *Falcon*, Han sees that the Resistance fighters are in trouble. First Order troops had launched a counterattack. He knows that if they don't help the X-wing fighters, the Resistance will be finished. Han and Chewbacca take a supply of detonators into an access tunnel and plant them along the columns that support the oscillator. But Han spots Kylo Ren storming across a walkway, and he steps out to confront his son. As Finn and Rey watch from an access tunnel above, Kylo Ren ignites his lightsaber into the chest of Han Solo as way to end his inner conflict.

Enraged, Chewbacca fires on Kylo Ren and then detonates the explosives lining the columns. As the tunnel begins to tremble and fall apart, Rey and Finn run to the snowy forest.

Meanwhile, Resistance fighters, seeing the new hole blown into the oscillator, escalate their attack. Poe successfully penetrates the hole to blow up to the oscillator from within, causing the Starkiller base to begin to collapse.

As Finn and Rey rush through the trees, the chaotic crackle of Kylo Ren's lightsaber stands in their way. Rey pulls her blaster, but Kylo used a Force push to slam her against a tree. Finn rushes to her side, but as he checks on her, Kylo Ren approaches. Pulling out the lightsaber Maz Kanata had given him on Takodana—the one he had promised to deliver to Rey, the one that had belonged to Luke Skywalker and his father before him—Finn ignites the lightsaber and faces Kylo.

Recognizing the lightsaber, Kylo demands he hand it over, saying it is his. But Finn refuses and clashes sabers with the sinister Knight of Ren. Kylo beats away Finn's advances, causing Finn to loose his lightsaber. Kylo corners Finn against a tree and burns his shoulder. As Finn falls forward, Kylo slashes him across the back.

Reaching out with the Force, Kylo attempts to retrieve the lightsaber, but it flies out of the snow and whips past him—into the hands of Rey. She ignites the blade and races toward Kylo, determined to make him pay for what he had done to Han Solo, to Finn, to the Resistance, and to her. She struggles against her foe as he backs her to the edges of a crevasse in the swiftly destabilizing planet.

Kylo tells her that she needs training, that he could teach her the ways of the Force. Reminded of something Maz Kanata had told her on Takodana, Rey closes her eyes and embraces the Force. Strengthened, Rey fights back, gaining the advantage in the fight. With several deft blows, she severely injures Kylo, leaving him incapacitated and lying in the snow. As Rey stands over him contemplating her next move, a great tremor splits the ground, separating them.

Realizing there is nothing else she can do, Rey leaves the fight and rushes to Finn's side. Suddenly a light shines through the trees—Chewbacca in the *Falcon* has come to rescue them. The *Falcon* lifts from the planet moments before it explodes.

Back on D'Qar, Rey readies herself for a new mission. With the map to Luke Skywalker complete, she and Chewbacca board the *Millennium Falcon* headed for previously uncharted space and a new adventure—one that could bring balance to the galaxy once again.

OPPOSITE: Rey wields Anakin Skywalker's lightsaber. **ABOVE:** As Starkiller Base's core crumbles, a chasm is created separating Kylo Ren from Rey.

How It Was Filmed

The final lightsaber battle in the snow was actually filmed on a soundstage. Many steps were taken to create the look of a forest. Before the filming of the battle began, huge branches of spruce forty-five feet long were acquired and piled up outside the stage. Eventually, these massive branches would be brought into the filming area, lifted up, and secured to the soundstage ceiling. Initially, twelve actual trees were brought into the location, but before filming of the sequence began, the number rose to 180 trees.

The set was built on layers, to give the illusion of an actual forest. First the trees were put into position, and then the floor was covered with sand bags to give the forest floor a natural appearance. On top of the bags, ground cover was laid out. Finally, buttresses were put in place.

ABOVE: J.J. Abrams gives direction amid the trees and snow of Starkiller Base while Domhall Gleeson (General Hux), snowtroopers, and crewmembers look on.

In order for actors and stunt doubles to perform safely on the set, clear areas for fighting and soft areas for landing were included. The fight choreography was designed to work with the details of the set.

Most of the trees used in the scene were real, but a rubber tree was used for impacts. Crews also created foam logs and bark textured mats. The mats were wrapped around real trees so stunt performers would not get hurt.

A gully ran along one end of the set. It was carved by the production's scuptor, Dave Hodges. To give the massive scene the final touch of a winter landscape, a company called Snow Business was brought in to spray paper snow everywhere.

Once all these components were in place, filming began and the desolate, wooded landscape of Starkiller Base was brought to life as the backdrop for the pivotal lightsaber fight sequence between Kylo Ren and Rey.

DUEL ON STARKILLER BASE
BUILDING INSTRUCTIONS

BOX

- Fold piece B1 as shown and glue it to the inside top edge of piece B2.
- Mountain fold the tabs on pieces B3 and B4 and glue them to B1 and B2 as shown above to form the box.

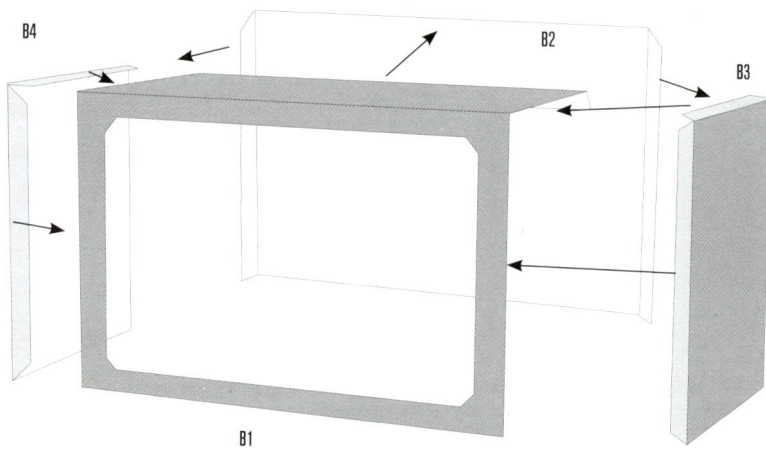

B4

B2

B3

B1

NOTE: For the following instructions, use pieces from the sheets labeled "Duel on Starkiller Base."

SCENE FRAME

- Valley fold the tabs on pieces 1, 2, 4, and 5.

- Glue each side of piece 5 to a side tab on pieces 2 and 4 as shown, so the printed surfaces all face in.

- Glue piece 1 to the bottom of the structure formed by pieces 2, 4, and 5, so all printed surfaces are facing in.

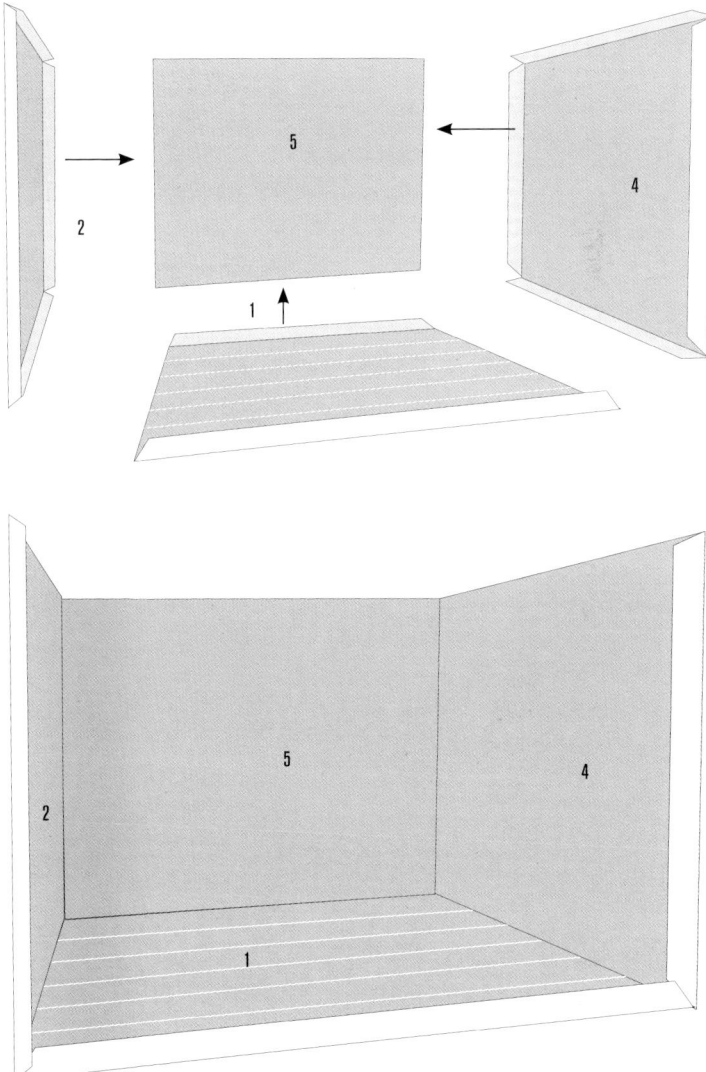

- Mountain fold the tabs on piece 6. Align the bottom tab with the line marked farthest back on piece 1 so it is next to piece 4. Glue in place. Then, gently fold piece 8 back and glue the side tab to piece 4, aligning with the deepest line on that piece.

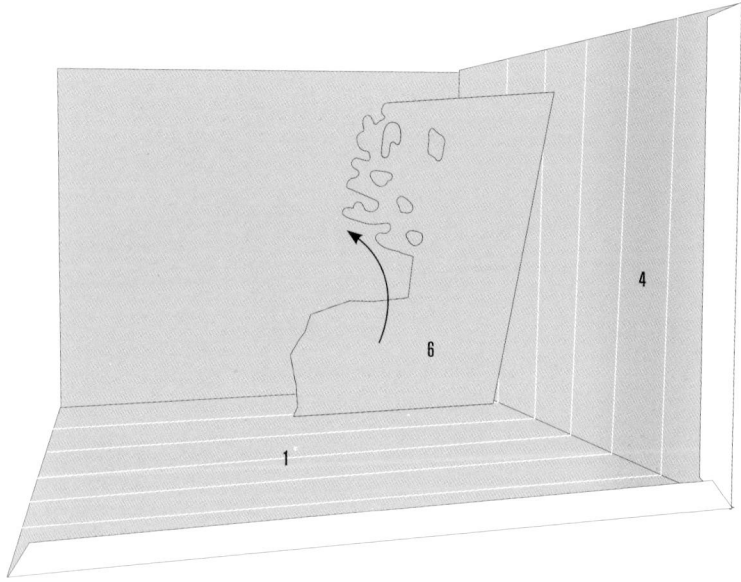

- Repeat this step with piece 7, aligning it so it is next to piece 2.

- Mountain fold the tabs on piece 8. Align the bottom tab with the line on piece 1 just in front of piece 6. Fold piece 8 back and glue it to the side of piece 4.

- Repeat this step with piece 9 so it is aligned with the line just in front of piece 7 and attached to piece 2.

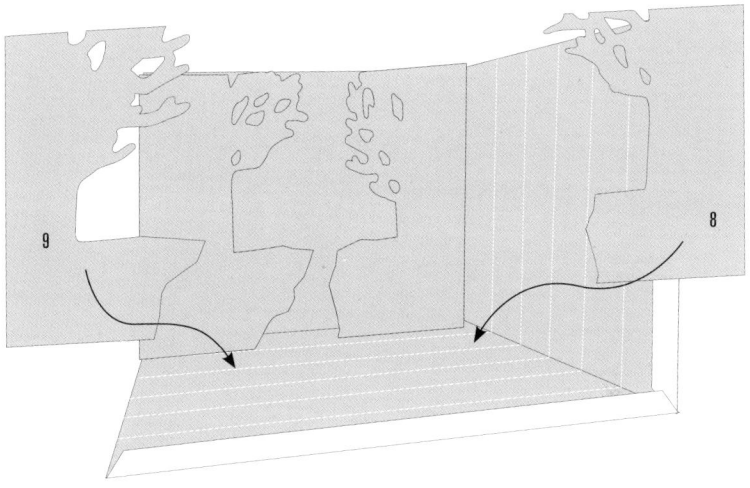

- Mountain fold the tabs on pieces 10 and 11. Align the bottom tabs with the third line on piece 1. Glue piece 10 so it is flush with the side of piece 4, and glue piece 11 flush with piece 2. Gently fold pieces 10 and 11 back and glue the side tabs to piece 4 and piece 2.

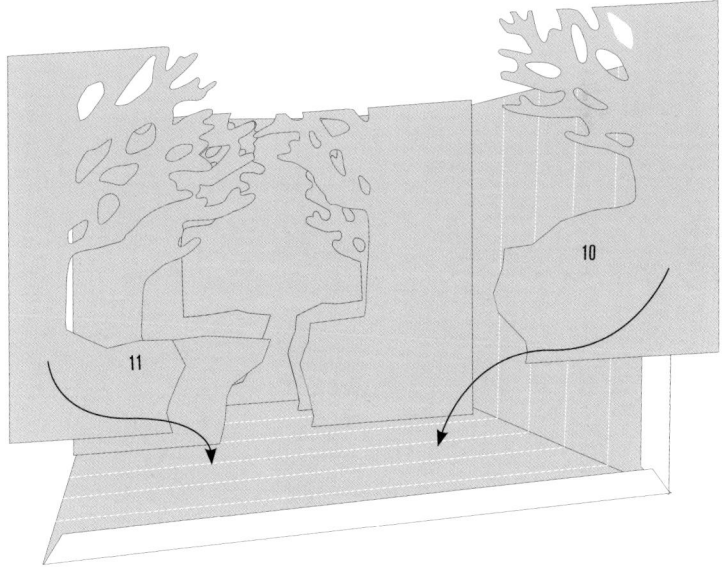

- Repeat this step with pieces 12 and 13, as well as pieces 14 and 15, aligning them so they are next to piece 2 and piece 4 as shown.

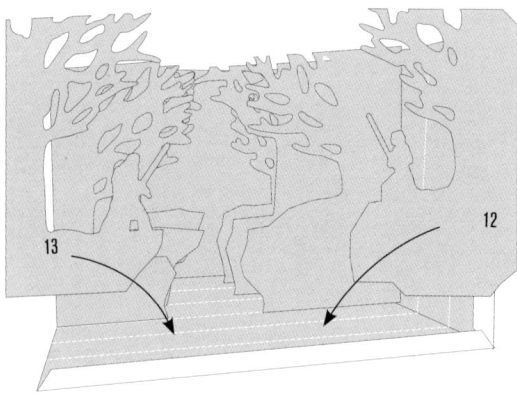

- Take piece 16 and round the log shape and branches slightly by rolling those areas over a pencil. Then mountain fold the tabs. Glue the bottom tabs to the first line on piece 1 and the side tab to piece 4 as shown.

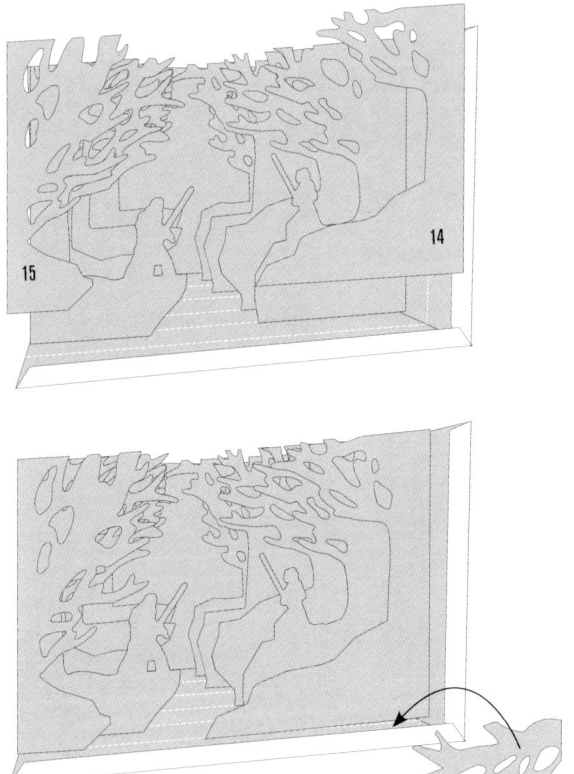

LOGS

- Assemble pieces 17 and 18 to form cylinders as shown.

- Slide piece 17 through the top hole in piece 4 so it extends across the scene and touches piece 1. Add some glue to the external side of piece 4 to hold the log in place.

- Slide piece 18 through the bottom hole in piece 4 so it extends across to scene and insert it into the hole on piece 2. Add some glue to the external side of piece 2 and piece 4 to hold the log in place.

17

18

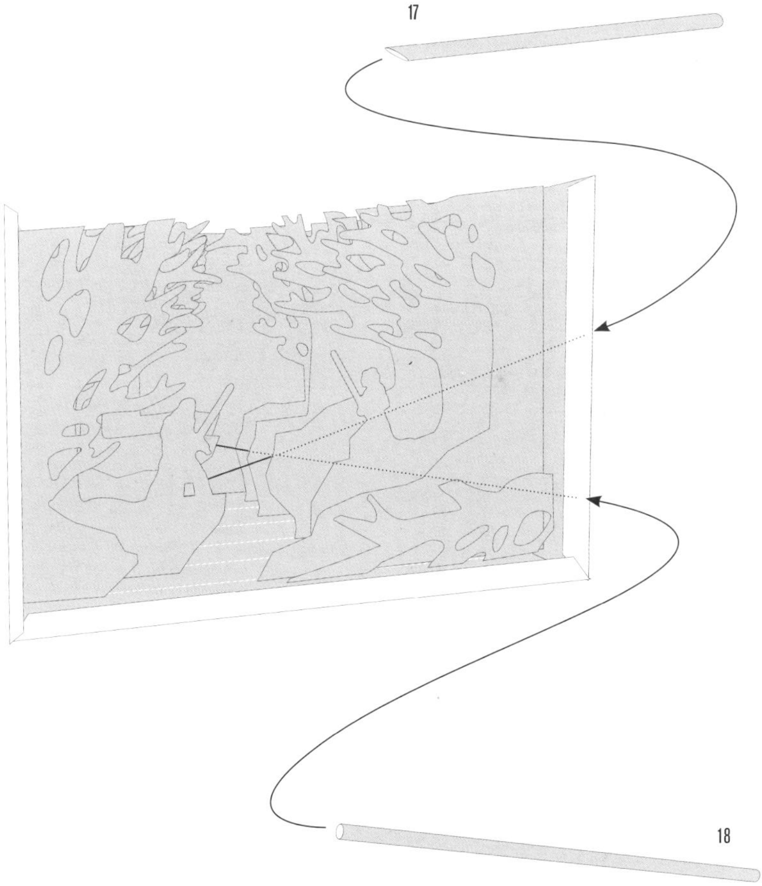

FINAL ASSEMBLY

- Valley fold the tabs on piece 3.

- Glue piece 3 to the top of the structure formed by pieces 2, 4, and 5. This completes the scene frame.

- Insert the scene frame into the outer box so the scene shows through the opening. Glue the tabs highlighted in yellow to the inside of the window of the box.

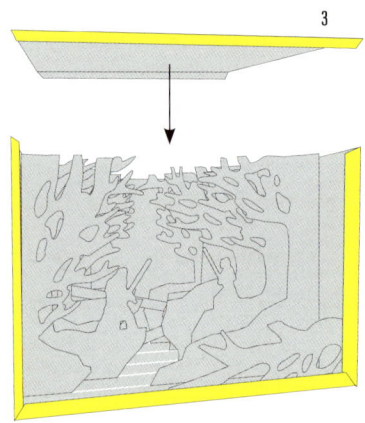

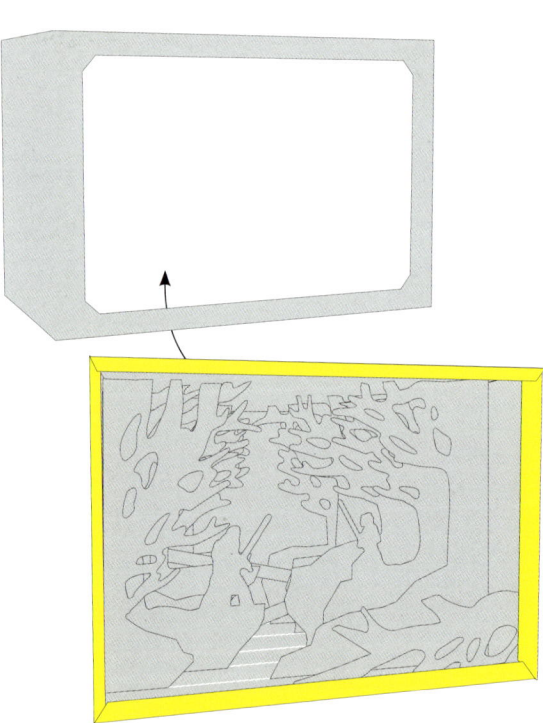

INSTRUCTIONS FOR BATTERY REPLACEMENT

The audio module includes three AG10 batteries (2 x 1.5V = 3.0V).
If the audio does not play, you may need to replace the batteries.
Batteries should be replaced by adults only. Batteries are small and
could possibly be ingested, so a child should never use this product
unless the battery compartment has been properly secured. To
replace the batteries, loosen the screw on top of the module and
remove the battery door. Remove the exhausted batteries and install
new batteries using the correct polarity displayed on the battery door.

Only use batteries of the same or equivalent type AG10. Do
not mix old and new batteries. Do not mix alkaline, standard
(carbon-zinc), or rechargeable (nickel-cadmium) batteries. Do
not use rechargeable batteries or attempt to recharge non-
rechargeable batteries. Do not short-circuit the supply terminals.